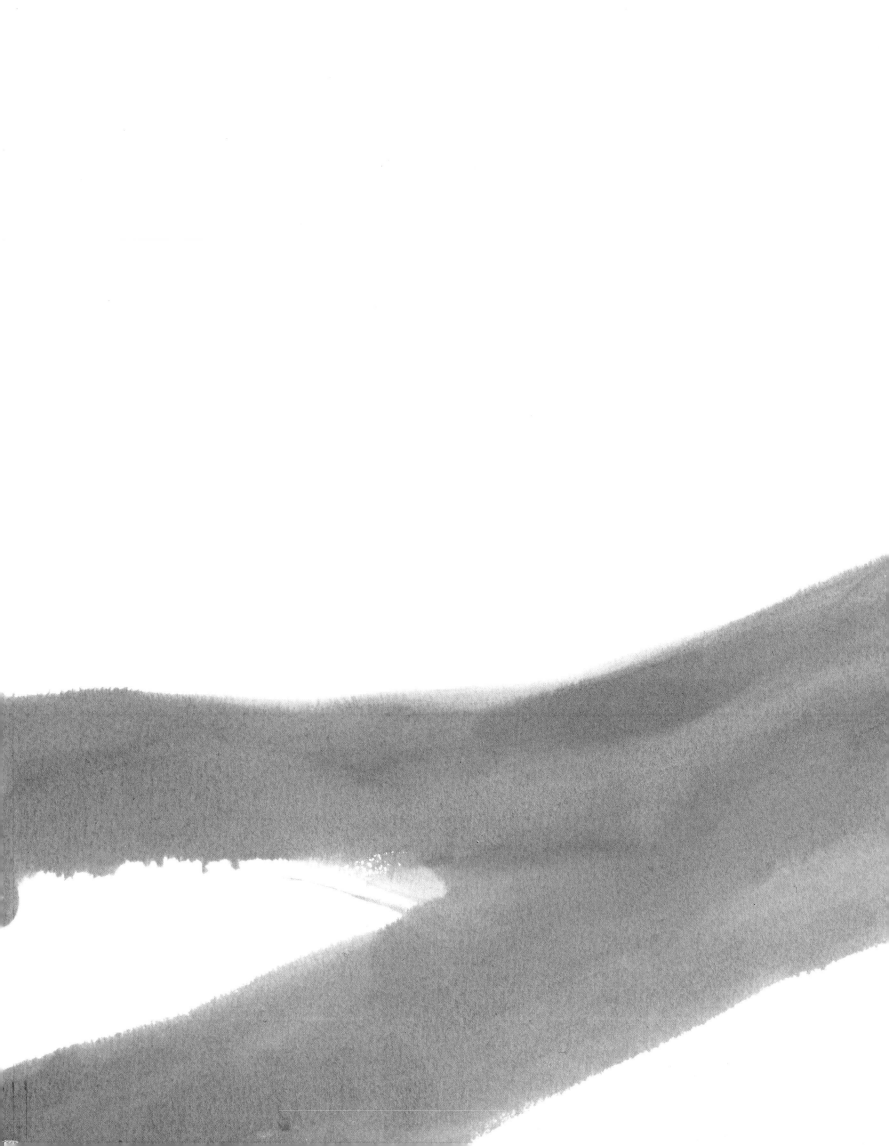

MONSTERS
Creatures of Mystery

By Nancy Christensen
Illustrated by Pamela Baldwin Ford

Platt & Munk, Publishers/New York
A Division of Grosset & Dunlap

For Jonathan, Kirsten and Alexis — three very special monsters.

TABLE OF CONTENTS

YOUR BASIC MONSTER ● For thousands of years, the Chinese have flown a flag emblazoned with an "imaginary" dragon. Who ever suspected that, early in the twentieth century, similar dragons would be discovered on a Pacific island? Every school child knows the fears and fantasies of our ancestors concerning the existence of fabulous creatures in the oceans. Yet, in 1977, a sea monster was actually netted off the coast of New Zealand. And can you imagine a creature less likely to exist (undetected for some 2,500 years) than the mountain gorilla? Truly, a myth come true! As more and more unchartered wilderness is explored, scientists are discovering that many of the legendary creatures in literature and folklore really exist.

There are still many monsters at large. What makes a monster? In order to achieve "monster" status, certain standards must be met. No single monster will boast all of the following traits, but each one is characterized by at least several.

Monsters don't live in cities. They inhabit inaccessible mountains, impenetrable forests, remote islands, and deep seas. Once they are familiar to man, however, they lose the aura of mystery that separates creatures from monsters. Lions are not monsters — simply because we know where they live, what they eat, and what they look like — not because they don't inspire fear and wouldn't be likely to tear someone to pieces at a moment's notice.

Mysteriousness alone does not a monster make, nor does ugliness. If you have ever seen an enlarged photograph of an insect, you will understand why enormous size is an important feature for monsters. Monsters smell foul; many species are described as "stinking like rotten eggs." They possess enormous strength and are generally carnivorous, or meat eaters. When hungry enough, some of them are not averse to carrying off a human or two. Predictably, monsters are nocturnal; most sightings are reported during the evening hours.

However, not all monsters are menacing; some are just mischievous or quite shy. This is often the case with those that are a curious combination of animal and human. Traditionally, these are excessively hairy, often carry weapons, and are known to discard the intestines of animals before eating them.

An element of loyalty to humans, even sometimes a romantic attachment, has been known to make monsters endearing. Think of some of the fictional monsters you have seen

in movies and read about in books. Had King Kong chosen to climb the Empire State Building or the World Trade Center clutching a handsome young man, it is likely that he would have gained considerably less sympathy.

But most of all, monsters are elusive. Quite undetected, they inhabit areas hunted by man, leaving only a smattering of clues to whet the appetite. They swim in our lakes, climb our mountains, and dot the earth with mysterious footprints. Monsters are alive and well.

LIFE-GIVING SEAS • Deep in the impenetrable, dark waters of the ocean live the largest animals ever known to have existed. The seas teem with intelligence and life grown to gigantic proportions and strength never encountered by man. Only through chance events — such as a whale that vomits an undigested meal of giant squid, or a storm that washes ashore an 8-foot jellyfish with 200-foot tentacles — do we get a hint of the strange and awesome creatures that live under thousands of pounds of water pressure in the seas.

Some of the most intelligent and civilized forms of life inhabit the seas. When a dolphin becomes ill, other dolphins take turns holding it above water, allowing it to breathe until it recovers, sometimes several days later. And when a mother whale gives birth, it chooses a "godmother" to help it care for its infant. It is believed that the sound patterns (or language) of some sea creatures will one day be decoded, and that humans may be able to talk with them.

The largest known mammal, the blue whale, has a recorded length of 113.5 feet, weighing between 150 and 170 tons. The tongue alone of one blue whale weighed 6,000 pounds! The carcasses of eleven new species of whale, never before seen by man, have been washed up on beaches.

The giant squid (never captured alive) is like a ten-legged octopus, with an arm span of 50 feet. And just try to imagine tortoises weighing over 500 pounds, 90-foot sea worms, 1,000-pound clams, and a 3,000-pound manta ray that is 22 feet wide and 17 feet long.

Monsters beyond our wildest speculation must live in the oceans. In 1930, near the Cape of Good Hope, the 6-foot larva of a giant sea serpent was caught in a fishing net. Scientists estimate that the full-grown adult would have reached a length of up to 180 feet!

A boatload of experts from Sandy Hook Marine Laboratories witnessed a transparent sea monster in 1963, 40 to 50 feet in length and 5 to 7 inches in width. None could begin to identify the species. What is particularly bizarre about this sighting is that it took place a short distance from New York City. The monster was again seen off the coast of Philadelphia — hardly unchartered territory.

The life-giving potential of the earth's waters and its function as an experimental laboratory for new and exaggerated species should come as no surprise, since all forms of animal life, including man, evolved from the sea.

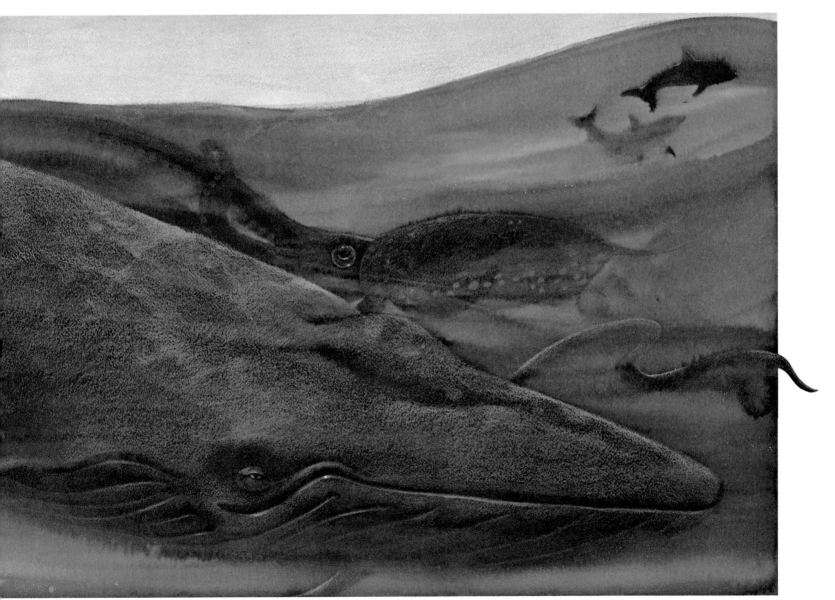

THE FIRST MONSTERS ● Hundreds of millions of years ago, all creatures lived in the sea. As the earth changed, they also changed, or evolved, to survive in their new environment. Some learned to live in fresh water; others flopped about in the mud, and finally crawled out of the slimy swamps to venture forth on land. Their fins developed into feet, and they grew strong legs for chasing their prey. Teeth sharpened for ripping chunks of raw meat. Then, for one hundred and thirty million years, the earth was ruled by monsters.

Spiders, dragonflies, cockroaches, and other insects shared the earth with these dinosaurs and kept the secret for another 70 million years, until the first fossilized skeletons were discovered in 1811 by a little girl in England. Ever since, man has fantasized about coming face to face with dinosaurs.

Coelacanths are ancient fish that were believed to have died out 70 million years ago with the last dinosaur. Yet, in 1938, and again in 1952, coelacanths were caught off the coast of Africa. Similarly, you might wonder if, one day, from a peaceful lake or desolate swamp, the head of a monster will emerge, where it has been lying in wait.

KOMODO DRAGONS • Imagine the terror experienced by an airplane pilot who was forced to make an emergency landing on a little island in the Pacific, only to find himself face to face with dragons! Who would ever have guessed that varanid lizards, thought to be extinct for over 60 million years, were living together with every order of poisonous snake known to man on an uninhabited Indonesian island?

It is believed that these prehistoric creatures survived by swimming from Australia to Komodo Island, a sanctuary from their natural enemies, the tiger and the wild dog.

If these "dragons" were seen centuries ago, it is possible that their long, flickering, yellow forked tongues inspired the age-old image of fire shooting from the mouths of mythical dragons.

LOCH NESS MONSTER • The first recorded sighting of the Loch Ness monster dates back to A.D. 565 in Scotland, where it was written that St. Columba happened into a group of local residents who were burying the victim of a sea monster from Loch (Lake) Ness. When one of Columba's companions went to recover the victim's boat, the monster reappeared and was frightened back by Columba's sign of the cross and order to retreat.

Since then, historians have repeatedly told of sightings of the mysterious creatures. "Nessie" generally surfaces when the lake is placid, and the disturbance it causes in the water indicates that it is of immense proportions. The monster is of a dark charcoal-brown color, with virtually no definition separating its head from the long giraffe-like neck. It has

three humps on its back, a long blunt tail, and four large fins. The monsters apparently travel under water in herds, and on occasion, more than one have been sighted at the same time. The length of one monster is estimated at 15 to 50 feet, and it is possible that two or more swimming together give the illusion of one incredibly long monster.

Loch Ness is 22 miles long and 970 feet deep, with 2,000-foot mountains surrounding it. Its inky black waters are believed to have been part of the ocean until the Ice Age, when land masses cut it off from the sea. It is possible that large sea creatures were trapped in Loch Ness and, not unlike sharks and many other species, adapted, or acclimated, themselves to fresh water.

Underwater specialists have used sophisticated equipment to gain information about Nessie. Echo sounders, by sending out high-frequency sounds and collecting their echoes, have sketched the outline of a 50-foot creature moving about 480 feet below the surface of Loch Ness at speeds up to 17 miles per hour. Underwater cameras have produced tracings of two 20- to 30-foot monsters with pronounced humps. These photographs have been proved genuine by America's National Aeronautical and Space Administration (N.A.S.A.) and the British Museum of Natural History. The most dramatic underwater photograph, taken only 8 feet from the monster, shows a hideous face with large nostrils and two tubes protruding from the top of the head.

Unfortunately, despite strong evidence that the Loch Ness monster may be a survivor of the prehistoric plesiosaur species, no one has been able to produce a carcass to confirm once and for all the true identity of Nessie. Since little vegetation grows in the cold, acidic waters of Loch Ness, bacteria is not plentiful. As a result, the carcasses do not rot and form gases that would cause them to float to the surface. Instead, the bodies presumably sink to the bottom of the deep lake, where they slowly become covered with mud. Thus, according to local legend, "the loch never gives up its dead."

The creature also manages to avoid close scrutiny by rarely surfacing when the lake's waters are not peaceful. Although a boat once actually collided with one of the creatures — it was probably ill or dazed — any noise or activity generally sends it rapidly back to the lake bottom, where it remains hidden in ridges and caverns.

Some of the more popular theories about Nessie's identity include one that it is a whale, which is doubtful because of its long neck and small head. Also, whales cannot climb out of the water, as Nessie has been known to do, and they must surface frequently in order to breathe.

It isn't likely that the monster is an enormous seal, since seals spend too much time ashore. Giant sea cows seem to be out of the question, since they cannot breathe under water and need vegetation for food. The theory that three giant turtles swimming together might give the illusion of a monster is interesting, except that turtles cannot live in such cold water and must surface regularly to breathe. Could it be a giant eel giving a hump-like illusion? The size makes it very unlikely.

Then what is Nessie? "The beastie in the loch" has provided mystery for over 1,400 years. For many years, men and women have set watch on the shores of the lake for a glimpse of the creature. Hoaxers have faked photographs, carcasses, footprints — probably the most famous being molded footprints made with the stuffed foot of a hippopotamus, which was part of an umbrella stand. Sightings have been fabricated to attract tourists, and silenced to avoid ridicule.

Nessie is probably of the same species as other monsters sighted in high mountain lakes in many of the United States, Canada, South America — even in Loch Morar, only 40 miles from Loch Ness. Descriptions of these creatures bear a striking resemblance to the skeletal fossils of Elasmosaurus, a member of the plesiosaur family of marine reptiles that existed in this part of Scotland 65 million years ago.

Plesiosaurus

In 1977, Japanese fishermen netted the 2-ton carcass of a 32-foot sea monster off the coast of New Zealand — probably a saltwater version of the Loch Ness monster before its Ice-Age acclimation to fresh water. Because the men feared that the rancid carcass would contaminate the shipful of fish they had caught, they sketched and photographed the creature, cut off a flipper, and threw it back into the ocean. Imagine their embarrassment when they returned to shore and realized they had thrown away the most exciting piece of scientific evidence of the century! When they went back to the scene, numerous searches of the area failed to locate the carcass.

The netting of the New Zealand monster brings to mind ancient world maps drawn in the 1500's, showing the seas inhabited by monsters. Those resembling whales and giant squid we can accept, but sea monsters rearing their terrible heads? Is it possible that our ancestors were not superstitious fools, but were witnesses to prehistoric survivors that still dwell in the oceans . . . and placid lakes of Scotland?

GENTLE GIANTS • Although artifacts and literary references indicate sightings of gorillas in the year 700 B.C., the first lowland gorilla was encountered by an expedition in 1856.

These peaceful creatures live in small families, eating only vegetation. Because of their enormous size (adult males grow as tall as 5 feet 8 inches and weigh 450 to 600 pounds), they have earned the nickname "the gentle giants." Mountain gorillas are among the most intelligent animals; test scores have indicated that some have IQ's as high as young children.

Even today, it is virtually impossible to detect signs of the existence of the gorilla in the jungle. Gorillas have an uncanny instinct for detecting the presence of humans, and they are able to disappear without a sound or sight. When they die, the thickness of the jungle shields their decaying bodies; other gorillas make doubly certain they are not discovered by hiding the corpses under grass and leaves. The skeletons are later devoured by other animals.

The existence of the mountain gorilla wasn't discovered until the early twentieth century, although for the preceding 50 years, its habitat had been regularly explored. And, more than 65 years ago, skeletons were discovered of what appears to be still another species of gorilla. Although scientists are fairly certain that this "pygmy gorilla" exists, it has yet to be seen alive by any human. This is particularly distressing, since the mountain gorilla is now in danger of extinction, and the pygmy gorilla (and possibly other species, as well) may become extinct before being discovered.

YETI • If you have ever played the game "Telephone," you'll understand how Yeti got the name "The Abominable Snowman." In 1921 a British explorer in Nepal discovered tracks in the snow and was told by his Sherpa guides that these were the footprints of "the wild man of the snows." He immediately telegraphed this message to India, but because of poor translation and garbled transmission, the message read, "filthy, dirty or smelly snowman." The newspapers wasted no time announcing the discovery of an "Abominable Snowman," and this is what it has come to be called.

The first allusion to this monster appears in Chinese manuscripts as early as 200 B.C. Yet the first reported sighting by a Western explorer was in 1903, when William Knight stood less than 20 feet from a pale yellow creature, almost 6 feet tall, with amazing muscular development. It had sparse hair on its face and was carrying what appeared to be a primitive form of bow. After five minutes, the creature, which the natives of the Himalayas refer to as Yeti, ran down the hill at tremendous speed.

The Abominable Snowman presents unique problems for monster fans. If it didn't just happen to inhabit the highest mountain in the world, it would probably remain a secret chapter in Far Eastern folklore. However, many expeditions to Mount Everest by Western explorers have resulted in numerous reported sightings, predominently of enormous footprints. Amazing tales from native guides further arouse speculation about these mysterious creatures.

What is Yeti? Local legend holds that murderers who escaped from prison many years ago made their homes in the mountains, mated with wild beasts, and over the generations have become flesh- and man-eaters. When they are particularly hungry and lustful, they sneak into villages and steal oxen and women.

Curiously, it is not unusual to find, in the immediate vicinity of Yeti footprints, the freshly removed intestines of mouse hares and other animals — an eating habit that is unusual for animals, yet quite common for humans.

The langur monkey has probably inspired some reported sightings. And it is possible

that the orangutan, which actually inhabited the Himalaya Mountains 250,000 years ago, is still at large in this area. Fossil evidence attests that another form of ape called Gigantopithecus lived in northern India millions of years ago, and records show signs of its existence in China only 750,000 years ago. And just try to imagine how you would describe a gorilla if you had never seen one before and suddenly came face to face with one in a mountain wilderness!

The Tibetan blue bear is so rare and elusive it has never been seen alive by Western man. It is possible that many Yeti sightings are the result of seeing this bear, or another equally shy animal. Every year the National Geographic Society reports on the discovery of about fifty new species of mammals. If the gorilla was able to remain a mystery for 2,500 years, it is not impossible that the Abominable Snowman has thus far managed to avoid scrutiny.

23

Although many mysterious enormous footprints are probably the result of the sun melting much smaller footprints, thus distorting them to gigantic proportions, this clearly is not the case in the perfectly exposed photograph of an obviously fresh print taken in 1951 by Eric Shipton, a member of the Everest Reconnaissance Expedition.

There are other bits of evidence that make it impossible to deny the existence of some mysterious creature in the Himalaya Mountains. We can hardly explain away a lair that was found in a cave — a huge nest made of juniper branches that had been pulled from the ground with the roots still attached — clearly a superhuman feat.

What about the monastery in the Himalayas that claims to have a mummified hand and the hair-covered skull of what appears to be a Yeti? And is it likely that some of the world's most highly respected mountaineers would confuse a bear for an unidentified creature?

While there is no doubt that some of the sightings are hoaxes, and others may be superstitious folly, if there is even one real footprint . . .

ALMAS ● On the Russian side of the Himalayas, the Abominable Snowman is known as Almas — a more sophisticated creature than Yeti. Native Russians think that Almas are surviving members of the ancient Neanderthal race of man.

For many years, scientists believed that Neanderthal man was an unsuccessful evolution — or development of man — that died out as the later Cro-Magnon man flourished. Recent research shows that it is more likely that Neanderthals mated with Cro-Magnons and, therefore, are still genetically present in modern man.

It is possible that a pure breed of Neanderthal still exists in some of the more impenetrable and isolated parts of the earth. These primitive men are known to have understood the

domestic use of fire and carried hunting weapons. They were probably the first to believe in an afterlife; consequently, they buried their dead with worldly possessions. Fossil evidence indicates that Neanderthals did exist in Russia 50,000 years ago — in precisely the same place where Almas have been sighted.

A Russian doctor was once called to a small mountain village where a "wild man" was captured. The doctor reported that the creature was less than six feet tall, was hairy everywhere except on his face, and made noises like an animal. He concluded that the creature was almost certainly a survivor of the Neanderthal race, and was probably driven into the mountains generations ago.

Unlike the bear- and langur-like sightings of Yeti, natives report a different kind of encounter with Almas. One report involves the discovery of an Almas woman breast-feeding a human child. Another sighting describes hunters returning to their campsite to find Almas warming themselves by a campfire. (It is important to note that most animals are afraid of fire, and do not use fire to warm themselves. This is distinctly human behavior.)

In 1957 A. G. Pronin, a scientist from Leningrad University, was camping in Pamirs, when he was confronted by a manlike figure with long arms and covered with reddish gray hair. A few days later, he saw it again. When he made inquiries, he discovered that this creature was well-known to the natives.

An expedition in 1959 unsuccessfully attempted to locate this creature, but did discover artifacts, cave drawings, and evidence of the use of fire for heat — clear indications of primitive human occupancy!

SASQUATCH • If you happen to be in Washington, Oregon, California, the Mohave Desert, the Everglades, the Blue Ridge Mountains, or almost any of the southern United States, and you see a gigantic creature that is excessively hairy (except on the face, palms and soles of feet), with glowing eyes, heavy brow, a wide mouth, and square teeth — you've sighted a Sasquatch!

Thousands of Sasquatch footprints have been found, many of which have been made into plaster molds measuring 16 to 22 inches by 7 inches, resulting in the American nickname "Big Foot." Judging from the distance between prints and their depth, an adult Sasquatch would be 8 to 12 feet tall and weigh 400 to 800 pounds. It is virtually impossible for many of these prints to be hoaxes, since some have malformations that indicate injuries and birth defects. Only a foot specialist who understood the subtleties of bone structure and walking patterns would be able to create such a hoax — which is certainly unlikely.

Big Foot has been photographed; the most famous example is a film made in northern California by Roger Patterson of a Sasquatch walking through the woods. Its voice has been tape-recorded, revealing more articulate speech patterns than an ape's. And hair samples have been analyzed by scientists, indicating that it is humanoid — or, not unlike humans — but not human!

Sasquatches are believed to dwell in caves and to eat mostly mice, plants and berries. In the winter, when vegetation becomes scarce, it is presumed that they increase the amount of meat in their diet. Their eating habits are still something of a mystery, since their enormous size indicates that they should require abundant amounts of food, yet their habitat does not provide adequate vegetation.

Although it is possible that Neanderthal or Peking man migrated to North America during or after the Ice Age, American monster buffs speculate that Sasquatch is not man, and not ape, but a primitive manlike being — or "near man" — either an unsuccessful evolution or a strange result of crossbreeding.

It is interesting to note that in 1975, in the Atlanta Zoo, two apes with a greater chromosomal difference (difference in cells) than that between man and ape mated successfully and had healthy offspring. It had always been assumed that crossbreeding of this nature was a biological impossibility.

While Indian folklore is rich with allusions to Sasquatch, ranging from a kind of protector of tribes to a man-stealing giant, the first specific historical reference to it appeared in 1884. Newspaper accounts tell of a young, male, 4-foot-7-inch Sasquatch, weighing 127 pounds, captured near Yale, British Columbia by a crew of train workers. He was put in a cage and described as manlike, except for his extraordinary strength and the short, glossy hair all over his body. There is no subsequent newspaper report of "Jacko," as he was named, but stories conflict as to whether he escaped or became a circus exhibit for years to come.

In 1924, a prospector named Albert Ostman was carried off in his sleeping bag one night by an adult male Sasquatch. He was brought "home" — for whatever mysterious reason — and described the Sasquatch family as consisting of the 8-foot father, the 7-foot mother, a 7-foot teenage son, and an immature daughter. In spite of their excessive hairiness and technological simplicity, Ostman was struck by their human qualities. After six days, Ostman escaped, and he kept his kidnapping a secret for thirty-three years, for fear people would think he was crazy.

    In general, the Sasquatch appear to be nonaggressive, not hostile, not particularly curious, and without weapons. They have never been known to hurt a human, and yet, it has been reported that they will bombard humans with rocks when frightened or threatened.

    A dramatic example of this occurred in Ape Canyon, 75 miles north of Portland, Oregon, when a miner shot at an apelike creature that was peering out from behind a tree. Apparently, it was injured and ran off. Shortly thereafter, another encounter occurred. When the miner shot the creature three times in the back, the body fell into the canyon. That night, when the miners returned to their cabin, the cabin was assaulted for five hours by hurled rocks in what appears to have been a counterattack. Since there were no windows and the door was bolted, the miners were unharmed and were able to escape the next day.

Sasquatch skeptics theorize that the Sasquatch is a big bear, which can grow up to 10 feet tall and weigh over 1,700 pounds. This is not likely, however, since Sasquatch walks upright, has no snout, and appears to have apelike features. The footprints are clearly not bear tracks — Sasquatch has toes, not claws.

There is a very real fear that Sasquatch, whose sightings are less frequent each year, will become extinct before it is actually encountered by scientists. Both Washington State and Oregon have laws making it illegal to kill a Big Foot — in Skamania County, the fine is $10,000!

As always, local hoaxers complicate the search for real evidence. Although fake footprints can always be detected as such, their very existence lessens the credibility of real prints. One roadmender living in Sasquatch territory boasts of 16-inch feet he made of wood and attached to his boots. He also made a medium-sized pair for his wife, and a little pair for his child. Together, they romp through the wilderness, presumably providing thrills for tourists.

CREATURES OF MYSTERY ● Fossil evidence suggests that men taller than 12 feet actually lived millions of years ago. Cave drawings in Colorado show a giant human fighting a mammoth, an enormous mammal that has been extinct for 25,000 years. Another depicts Tyrannosaurus Rex, believed to have vanished from the earth at least 70 million years ago.

In 1932, prospectors discovered the mummified skeleton of a 14-inch man in a cave in Wyoming. X-rays and studies confirmed that the skeleton was that of a 65-year old human, although scientists were unable to determine during what era he had lived.

These discoveries raise questions about the missing links in the early evolution of man, and how many unsuccessful evolutions may yet be discovered . . . not to mention the discrepancy as to how primitive man, who lived on earth for about one million years, knew how to draw a long-extinct Tyrannosaurus!

Although the earth remains rich with secrets, not all of these secrets are buried. Mythical creatures have come to life in recent history — dragons on Komodo Island; the long-fantasized gorilla; new species of langurs; the Arabian oryx; giant pandas and pygmy hippopotomuses; and the coelacanth, secret survivor of the age of the dinosaurs. In fact, each year scientists discover about 50 new mammals, 100 new fish, 15 new reptiles, 15 new birds, and about 5,000 new insects.

As each creature is discovered, studied, and classified with a Latin name, it loses its monster status and becomes just another species of life on earth. And the monster hunt continues for more elusive creatures peeking out from the jungles and the seas. Imagine the terror of our ancestors if they could walk hand-in-hand with today's children through our zoos!